1. **This book may be kept three weeks. It is to be returned on / before the last date stamped below.**
2. **A fine of 20p will be charged for every week or part of week a book is overdue.**

	/ / JAN 2003	

D1381876

This edition first published in Ireland 1997
by The O'Brien Press Ltd.
20 Victoria Road, Dublin 6.
First published 1997 by Orchard Books
96 Leonard Street, London EC2A 4RH.
1 2 3 4 5 6 7 8 9 10
97 98 99 00 01 02 03 04 05 06
Copyright © Nicola Smee 1997
The right of Nicola Smee to be identified as the author and illustrator of this work has been
asserted by her in accordance with the Copyright, Designs and Patents Act, 1988.
A CIP catalogue record for this book is available from the British Library.
Printed in Italy
ISBN 0-86278-535-9

Freddie gets Dressed

Nicola Smee

O'BRIEN toddlers

My bear's bare
and so am I.
I think we'd better
get dressed.

Pants for me
and
pants for Bear.

T-shirt for me
and
T-shirt for Bear.

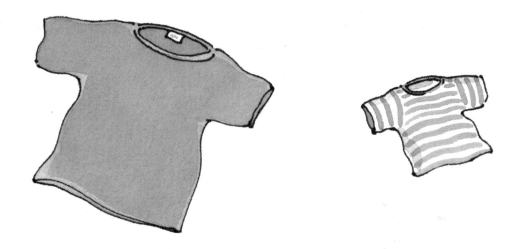

Socks for me
and
socks for Bear.

Trousers for
me and ...
I think a skirt for
Bear today.

Shoes for me
and
shoes for Bear.

Oh, no!
It's back to being
bare, Bear!